MW00583079

WHEN YOU WANT TO HIDE

Zoe's Time to Shine

EDWARD T. WELCH

Editor

JOE HOX

Illustrator

Bright white snow adorned the treetops and housetops of Mulberry Meadow.
It covered the icy pond and hidden burrows, and the mouse family's bungalow.

In their kitchen, stood Mama and Papa Mouse, wearing mouse-sized sweaters and stirring a pot of porridge. They could hear their daughter, Zoe, down the hall, singing in the shower, as she did most mornings before school.

"It's just the sweetest thing," said Mama. "That voice of hers!"

Papa agreed, scooping a spoonful of porridge into a bowl.

Soon Zoe arrived and had her fill of breakfast, hugged Mama and Papa goodbye, and scampered off to school.

Zoe's friend, Layla, eagerly watched from her window each weekday morning, waiting until the last possible second to step outside.

"It's *sooo* f-f-f-freezing!" Layla shivered, scampering down her steps.

"Let's sing to keep our minds off it!" exclaimed Zoe.

So the two friends sang along the way, tromping through the snow, smiling in the brisk morning air.

One by one, nearly all the animals from the meadow took their turn. Yet despite their many impressive talents, Zoe was *still* certain she'd get the lead.

When her turn came, Zoe marched on stage with supreme confidence. She said, "I'm ready, Ms. Franz." She then whispered, "I love *Maria's Dream*," and she gave Ms. Franz a wink.

Ms. Franz began playing the piano, and Zoe began singing. She sang so supremely off-key that behind her sparkly blue glasses, one of Ms. Franz's eyes appeared to be twitching, as her third eyelid rose higher and higher! Somehow Ms. Franz was able to finish the song . . . just barely. Then she croaked, "Uh, . . . thanks. Please take your seat."

After lunch, students fled to the auditorium for auditions. Zoe and Layla rushed to the front row.

"I wonder what song we'll sing," Layla said excitedly.

Then the drama teacher, Ms. Franz, emerged from behind the big red curtain. She was wearing a bright teal dress with sparkly sequins and a hot pink boa scarf. Her blue glasses sparkled in the spotlight.

"Attention!" she shouted. "Please take your seats. Welcome to the audition for *Maria's Dream!* When I call your name, you may join me on stage. You'll have one chance to audition, and the results will be posted tomorrow. Good luck to all!"

In homeroom, Zoe chatted with her friends.
"Which part are you trying out for, Zoe?" asked Freya.

Wide eyed, Zoe replied, "The lead of course!
I'll make the perfect Maria! I already know all her lines.
My aunt took me to see the musical last summer."

The next morning, Mama said to Zoe, "I'm excited for your audition! You know, Papa and I have never been very musical. We can hardly carry a tune! But we sure love when *you* sing!"

"I promise I'll tell you all about it tonight!" smiled Zoe. "I'm sure I'll have to practice every night and there'll be lots of rehearsals. Having the lead in a school musical is a *lot* of pressure!"

And off she went.

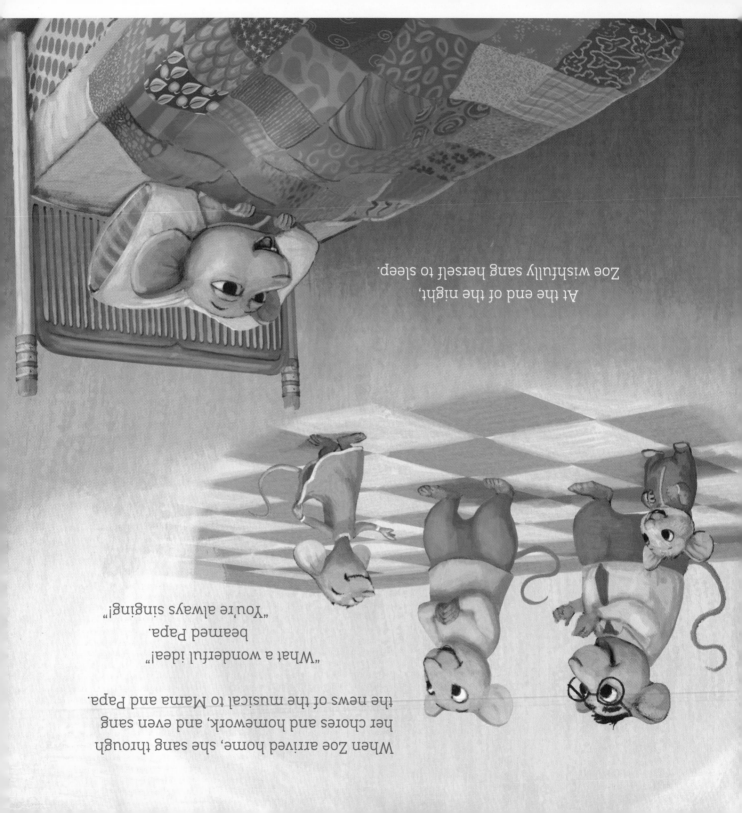

When Zoe arrived home, she sang through
her chores and homework, and even sang
the news of the musical to Mama and Papa.

"What a wonderful idea!"
beamed Papa.
"You're always singing!"

At the end of the night,
Zoe wishfully sang herself to sleep.

That afternoon on their way home, Zoe and Layla
sang every song they could think of: school songs, church
songs, movie songs, and made-up songs. It kept their
minds off the cold and helped them prepare for tomorrow.

As they sang together, Layla was pitch-perfect. Spot-on.
Sure to earn a place in the musical! But Zoe was often too
high or too low—too sharp or too flat. Never on key,
but always confident she'd steal the show.

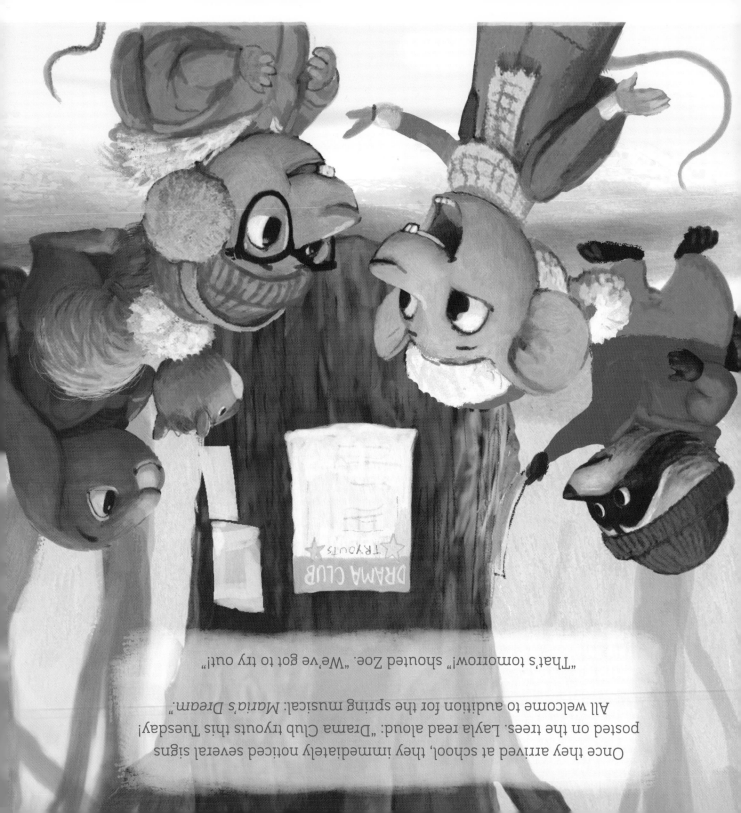

Once they arrived at school, they immediately noticed several signs posted on the trees. Layla read aloud: "Drama Club tryouts this Tuesday! All welcome to audition for the spring musical: *Maria's Dream*."

"That's tomorrow!" shouted Zoe. "We've got to try out!"

After everyone had tried out, Ms. Franz announced, "I'll post the results by morning. Because there aren't enough parts for everyone, consider serving in other roles— like stage crew, lighting, or costuming. I hope to see many of you back tomorrow!"

Zoe whispered to Layla, "Oh, we'll be back, all right!"

The next morning, Zoe woke extra early, showered extra fast, and arrived at Layla's with extra spunk. Layla opened the door and rubbed her eyes. "What *time* is it? I just woke up!"

"It's *time* to go see our names on the list! C'mon!" shouted Zoe. Layla hurried to get ready and was soon out the door.

But when they were within sight of the school,
they realized they weren't the only early birds.
A dozen other classmates were already reading
the list. Some were squealing and celebrating.
Others were turning away sniffling.

Once Zoe got close enough to read, she searched
for the part of Maria. *Where is it? Where is it?* she said
to herself, searching. And then she found it . . .
right next to Layla's name!

MARIA'S DREAM
ROLES

There must be some mistake, thought Zoe. She frantically searched the rest of the list. *I must be here somewhere!* But even when she got to the bottom, her name was still nowhere in sight. Deflated and embarrassed, she took a step back from the list.

This is impossible, thought Zoe. *I was supposed to be Maria.* She took another step back and another, until she backed right into . . . Ms. Franz!

"Good morning, Zoe! I was hoping to catch you! Listen, I'm wondering if you can help me with the lights for the show. Because you already know *Maria's Dream* so well, you'd be perfect! What do you say? Will you give it a try?"

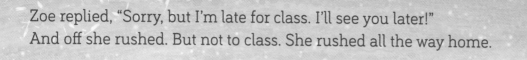

Zoe replied, "Sorry, but I'm late for class. I'll see you later!"
And off she rushed. But not to class. She rushed all the way home.

Zoe didn't sing along the way.

She didn't even smile.

She just ran and ran. And cried.

She quietly tiptoed into the bungalow, down the hall, and right into her closet. There she sat alone, wrapped in her purple blanket, remembering the audition and the list. Remembering homeroom and how confident she'd acted in front of her friends. *Now, what will they think of me? I can't possibly go back!*

"Zoe?" called Papa. "Is that you?"

He peeked behind the curtain. "Hi, there.
I'm surprised to see you. Did school get out early?"

"No," Zoe said sniffling.

"And I thought today was the big day!"

"It was."

"Ah," replied Papa, crouching next to Zoe. "May I join you?"

Zoe nodded yes. "I didn't even make the list," she cried.
"I told *everyone* I'd be on it and I'm not! And now Ms. Franz
wants me to run the lights instead!"

"I'm sorry, sweetie. I know how much that
meant to you, and how excited you were."

Zoe's pink nose sniffled.

"I understand why you want to hide."

"You do?" asked Zoe.

"Sure! It's hard to face others when we feel ashamed."

"I can't face them!" cried Zoe,
"I can't go back to school alone."

"I can go with you," Papa offered.

"No!" said Zoe. "That would be even more embarrassing."

Nodding his head, Papa said, "You know Zoe, once I had a very important meeting at work where my boss and everyone else thought my report was terrible. I wanted to run out of the room and hide. But I knew that would just make things worse. Instead, I thought about Jesus sitting right next to me, protecting me. When the right person is with us, it makes all the difference."

"But is Jesus really that close?" asked Zoe.

"Yes," said Papa. "The Great Book tells us that Jesus will never leave those he loves."

Zoe looked at Papa, "But how will Jesus being with me help when my friends make fun of me?"

Papa looked at Zoe's worried face and smiled. "Have you heard about the armor of God in the Great Book? Instead of hiding, you can think about how Jesus protects you with his own armor.

"Jesus wraps you in his belt of truth—that belt is all the promises he makes to you. He promises that he loves you and always forgives you when you need to be forgiven. He loves you no matter what your friends might think or say to you. He loves you when you are the best, and he loves you when you didn't make the spring musical.

"Then he dresses you in his breastplate of righteousness— it protects your heart when you feel like a failure. It is like a soldier's armor. It belongs to Jesus, and he lets you wear it. Even if you do something wrong, or even if someone doesn't like you—you will be safe. Jesus is your protection.

"Then there is the shield of faith. Believing that Jesus is with you protects you and makes you feel stronger. Jesus is very strong and he helps you feel strong too.

"When you go back to school, Jesus will be your shield so you can be all covered up—protected—and not have to hide in your closet."

Zoe looked a little less worried as she thought about walking back to school—not alone but with Jesus surrounding her.

"Here's a verse from the Great Book to remind you to look to Jesus," Papa said as he handed her a slip of paper.

THOSE WHO LOOK TO HIM ARE RADIANT; THEIR FACES ARE NEVER COVERED WITH SHAME.

Zoe read it and smiled,
"Mind if I take this back to school with me?"

"I think that's a great idea," said Papa.

With each step on her trek back to school,
Zoe prayed the words: *Those who look to him are
radiant, their faces are never covered with shame.*

And that's when she had an idea.

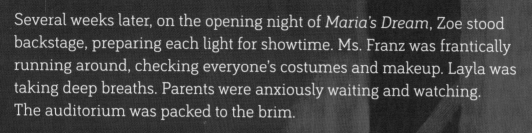

Several weeks later, on the opening night of *Maria's Dream*, Zoe stood backstage, preparing each light for showtime. Ms. Franz was frantically running around, checking everyone's costumes and makeup. Layla was taking deep breaths. Parents were anxiously waiting and watching. The auditorium was packed to the brim.

Zoe's heart raced with excitement as the music began playing and the drums began drumming. The entire cast took their places. Layla stepped into position on center stage.

Then it was Zoe's time to shine . . . the lights on all her friends! They all looked absolutely radiant.

> "Those who look to him are radiant;
> their faces are never covered with shame."
>
> Psalm 34:5

Helping Children Who Want to Hide

Think first about yourself and how you, like everyone else, still hide. We might not head for the closet, but we all have parts of us that we would prefer unseen. We don't want our sins to be seen, and, like Zoe, we don't want our mistakes or substandard performances to be on display. We are all concerned about our reputations. We don't want to be found unacceptable. We don't want to be among the left-out or passed-over. Wouldn't it be nice if our children could learn how to talk to Jesus about this rather than simply become more skilled at looking good on the outside?

Zoe felt ashamed. Shame is the experience of feeling unacceptable, less than others, or different. Sometimes we feel shame because we did something wrong and we can go to Jesus and ask for forgiveness, but shame is more often a result of being treated badly or simply believing we lack something and don't fit in.

Notice the language of shame: inferior, weak, inadequate, rejected, loser, nothing, different, ignored, failure, bullied, misfit, unattractive, stupid, unpopular, embarrassed, unwanted, stared at, last. Your child will inevitably feel some of these. The good news is that God knows that shame is part of the human condition, and he is doing something about it. Ever since Adam and Eve, people have been hiding, and God has been pursuing in love. He speaks words that build us up when we feel beyond repair and unacceptable.

Ways to Pursue with God's Love and God's Words

1 **"Pour out your heart" (Psalm 62:8).** Children need help putting their emotions into words. The more they speak, the better. You might say something like this, "God likes you to talk to him. He likes you to tell him what was great about your day, what was hard about your day, and where you want help. Let's do that now. Do you want to pray with me?" That's how we live with those we love, and that's how we live with our God who loves us. We speak what is on our heart. The psalms can guide us. Do you have a favorite psalm you can share with your children to help them put words on their experience? You could try Psalm 34, 91, 130, and many others.

2 **Connect their story to the Bible.** Your challenge as a parent is to connect the struggles of everyday life to God's good words. In this case, clothes could be that connection. Remind your children that Jesus gives us new clothes. Most children have some sense that the right clothes—the cool clothes—can bring some dignity to life. In the Bible, people could never be adequately covered by their own clothes. They needed God's covering. The Bible begins with do-it-yourself fig leaves and it ends with God's wedding garments (Revelation 19:7–8). In the meantime, think of Joseph's coat (Genesis 37:3), the priests' garments (Exodus 28), and the clothes God gives us for spiritual warfare (Ephesians 6:11–17). The beginning of the conversation might go like this. "Most of us have clothes we really like to wear. Do you have any favorite thing to wear?" "When we trust Jesus, he covers you so you don't have to hide. He gives you new clothes that are the best. He actually makes you look strong. Like a soldier. With spears and swords and armor and shields." Then, as Zoe's Papa did, go over Ephesians 6:11–17.

3 **Connect their story to Jesus.** The clothes show us that we are connected to a very important person. They are Jesus's clothes, and they remind us that he is the one who covers us. Shame leaves us feeling very alone. Covering reminds us that Jesus chose us for his team, and he is the King. Our own reputation is not enough. That's why we associate with those who we think are the right people. Children who are familiar with failure can know that Jesus's clothes mean that he is their friend—only best friends let us wear their clothes—and nothing could be better. Here's how the Bible explains it: "Thus says the LORD: 'Let not the wise man boast in his wisdom, let not the mighty man boast in his might, let not the rich man boast in his riches, but let him who boasts boast in this, that he understands and knows me.'" (Jeremiah 9:23–24 ESV). His words to us, "I have called you by name; you are mine" (Isaiah 43:1 NLT), are the best comfort after rejection and failure.

4 **And repeat.** Shame will not be fully solved today. Instead, the Spirit of God reminds us of these truths and teaches us more. He reminds us that Jesus actually knows what it's like to be unacceptable to the world. People even took his clothes. Then, having become like us, he invites us to join him when he rose from the dead and put on his kingly robes. He never leaves us alone, feeling as though we must hide.

The Good News for Little Hearts series is written by Jocelyn Flenders. Jocelyn is a graduate of Lancaster Bible College with a background in intercultural studies and counseling. She is a writer and editor living in the Philadelphia area.

New Growth Press, Greensboro, NC 27401
Text copyright © 2022 by Edward T. Welch
Illustration copyright © 2022 by Joseph Hoksbergen

All rights reserved. No part of this publication may be reproduced, stored in a retrieval system, or transmitted in any form by any means, electronic, mechanical, photocopy, recording, or otherwise, without the prior permission of the publisher, except as provided by USA copyright law.

Unless otherwise indicated, all Scripture quotations are taken from the Holy Bible, New International Version®, NIV®. Copyright © 1973, 1978, 1984, 2011 by Biblica, Inc.™ Used by permission of Zondervan. All rights reserved worldwide. www.zondervan.com. The "NIV" and "New International Version" are trademarks registered in the United States Patent and Trademark Office by Biblica, Inc.™

Scripture quotations marked (NLT) are taken from the Holy Bible, New Living Translation, copyright © 1996, 2004, 2015 by Tyndale House Foundation. Used by permission of Tyndale House Publishers, Carol Stream, Illinois 60188. All rights reserved.

Scripture quotations marked (ESV) are from the ESV® Bible (The Holy Bible, English Standard Version®), Copyright © 2001 by Crossway, a publishing ministry of Good News Publishers. Used by permission. All rights reserved. ESV Text Edition: 2016.

Cover/Interior Illustrations: Joe Hox, joehox.com

ISBN: 978-1-64507-284-3

Library of Congress Cataloging-in-Publication Data on file

Printed in India

29 28 27 26 25 24 23 22   1 2 3 4 5

Back Pocket Bible Verses

O my people, trust in him at all times. Pour out your heart to him, for God is our refuge.

Psalm 62:8 (NLT)

Stand firm then, with the belt of truth buckled around your waist, with the breastplate of righteousness in place . . . take up the shield of faith, with which you can extinguish all the flaming arrows of the evil one.

Ephesians 6:14, 16

Those who look to him are radiant; their faces are never covered with shame.

Psalm 34:5

Thus says the LORD: "Let not the wise man boast in his wisdom, let not the mighty man boast in his might, let not the rich man boast in his riches, but let him who boasts boast in this, that he understands and knows me."

Jeremiah 9:23–24 (ESV)

GOOD NEWS FOR LITTLE HEARTS

Back Pocket Bible Verses

WHEN YOU WANT TO HIDE

GOOD NEWS FOR LITTLE HEARTS

WHEN YOU WANT TO HIDE

GOOD NEWS FOR LITTLE HEARTS

WHEN YOU WANT TO HIDE

GOOD NEWS FOR LITTLE HEARTS

WHEN YOU WANT TO HIDE

GOOD NEWS FOR LITTLE HEARTS